One day Bungle, Zippy and George decide to water the flowers in the Rainbow garden. But Zippy's watering can has a hole in it, and Bungle drops his bucket. Will George have better luck?

rainbow

WATER, WATER, EVERYWHERE!

Written by Mike Butcher
Illustrated by Paul Crompton

Copyright © 1991 Thames Television Plc.
All rights reserved.
Published in Great Britain by World International Publishing Limited,
An Egmont Company, Egmont House PO Box 111,
Great Ducie Street, Manchester M60 3BL.
Printed in Germany. ISBN 0 7498 0320 7
REPRINTED 1992

A CIP catalogue record for this book is available from the British Library

"Here, Zippy!" calls Bungle. "See if you can catch this ball when I throw it!" Bungle, Zippy and George are all outside in the Rainbow garden.

"Do you want to play, too, George?"
Bungle asks.

"Er, no, thank you," says George. "I
think I'll water these flowers. They look
very thirsty!"

"I'll help you, George!" offers Zippy. "I'm very good at watering flowers," he boasts. Zippy soon finds a big, green watering can to use.

But Zippy is in such a rush to fill it up
that he splashes water all over himself!
By the time the watering can is full, Zippy
is wet through.

"Well, you've managed to water yourself, Zippy," grins Bungle. "Are you going to water the garden now?" Zippy carries the watering can over to the flowers.

But when he tries to water the flowers, nothing comes out of the watering can! Zippy is very puzzled . . . then he sees that the watering can is empty!

"Where has all my water gone?" gasps Zippy.

Bungle thinks he knows. "Look behind you," says Bungle. "You are clumsy, Zippy! You've spilt all your water on the path."

Zippy just can't understand it. "The watering can was full right up to the top before," he groans. "How could I have spilt all that water?"

Then George spots something. There is a hole in the bottom of Zippy's watering can! The water has trickled out through the hole onto the path!

"The watering can is no good," says Bungle. He fetches a big, red bucket. "I could water the whole garden with this big bucket," he chuckles.

Bungle turns on the tap and fills the bucket with water. He tries very hard not to spill any!

"I'll show you how to water the garden," he tells Zippy.

But the bucket is very heavy. Bungle can hardly carry it!

"Be careful, Bungle!" warns George. "I think your bucket is a little too full."

Bungle tries his best to carry the bucket across the garden, but he doesn't get far before he drops it. The water goes everywhere . . . except on the flowers!

"Well, you did say you could water the whole garden with that bucket, didn't you, Bungle-Bonce?" laughs Zippy. Poor Bungle has spilt even more water than Zippy did!

"Yuk!" moans Bungle. "My feet are all soggy now, from walking about on this wet grass." He is beginning to wonder if they will ever manage to water the flowers!

Just then, George has an idea.

"I won't be long," he tells Bungle and Zippy, and he rushes indoors.

A few minutes later, George comes back out into the garden with a small, yellow watering can.

"I thought we had a new watering can in the house," he smiles.

George fills up his watering can and goes over to the flowers. But before he can water them, Zippy notices a spot of rain in the air!

"Oh, no!" groans Bungle. "Now it's started raining! Let's go inside before my fur gets even more soggy than it already is. Come on, you two!"

Bungle, George and Zippy all run indoors as fast as they can to get out of the rain! It is not very long before it is pouring down outside.

"Well, that was a waste of time!" complains Zippy, looking at the garden through the window. "The rain is watering the flowers now. There was no need for us to do it after all."

"Yes," sighs Bungle, "but what are we going to do now? We can't play outside in the rain, or we'll get watered, too!"

"Don't worry," smiles George, holding up his yellow watering can. "I know how we can go on watering things without getting wet ourselves."